WON'T SOMEBODY PLAY WITH ME?

STORY AND PICTURES BY

STEVEN KELLOGG

DIAL BOOKS FOR YOUNG READERS · NEW YORK

First Pied Piper Printing 1976
Printed in Hong Kong by South China Printing Co.
COBE
6 8 10 9 7 5
WON'T *SOMEBODY* PLAY WITH ME? is published in a hardcover edition by
Dial Books for Young Readers, 2 Park Avenue, New York, New York 10016.
ISBN 0-8037-9612-9

"Happy birthday, Kim!"

"At five thirty when your daddy comes home from work."

"When do we open the presents?"

"While I'm waiting for five thirty,
I think I'll go down the hall to Timmy's apartment."

We can play witch and giant or famous generals or maybe we

can pretend that we have an orphanage for lost baby animals.

"Hello, Mrs. Lewis. Can Timmy come out?"

"I'm sorry, Kim, but Timmy has things to do inside for a while.
He'll telephone you later when he's finished."

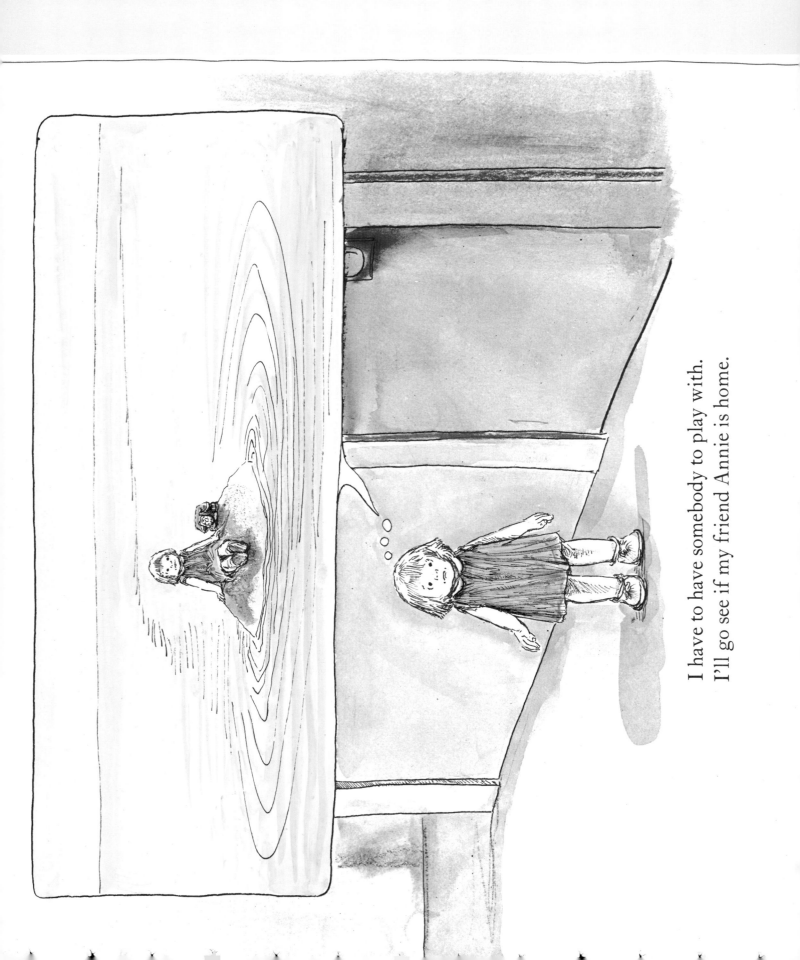

I have to have somebody to play with.
I'll go see if my friend Annie is home.

We can play superwomen or doctors or maybe we can run a famous restaurant and serve pineapple pancakes with bubblegum sauce.

"Hello, Mrs. Schwartz. Can Annie come out?"

"I'm sorry, Kim, but Annie isn't here right now.
She's gone to Timmy's house for the day."

Timmy and Annie! They're probably over there playing witch and giant together!

I'll go to Philip's house.

We can play ape family or spies or maybe we can pretend

that we're fierce, fat dinosaurs munching on bones.

"Hello, Mrs. Orfello. Can Philip come out?"

"I'm sorry, Kim, but Philip isn't here. He went over to Timmy's house for the day."

Timmy and Annie and Philip! They're over there together!
I bet they're playing ape family. And there's no one to play with me.

Well, if I were a queen sitting at a huge table piled with desserts and Timmy and Annie and Philip knocked on the door, I wouldn't let them in! I'd just sit there and stuff myself!

If I owned a toy store
filled with the best
toys in the world
and Timmy and Annie
and Philip knocked
on the door, I wouldn't
let them in. I'd just
play and play and play
by MYSELF!

If I had a rocket
and Timmy and Annie
and Philip called on
a walkie-talkie and said,
Can we come too?
I'd yell:
BLAST OFF!

And there I'd be...

all by myself...

But, boy, am I mad at Timmy!

And I'm really

That stupid Philip!

mad at Annie!

I might as well go home.

"Hello, Kim! How are you?"

"MAD!"

"Would you borrow a cup of sugar for me from Mrs. Lewis?"

"Do I have to?"

"Well, it's for your birthday cake."

"Okay."

21a

"Hello, Kim. We were just about to call you."

About the Author-Artist

Steven Kellogg is well known for his books for young children. His *Can I Keep Him?* was selected as one of the Best Books of the Year 1971 by *School Library Journal*, and his interpretation of Hilaire Belloc's *Matilda Who Told Lies and Was Burned To Death* was chosen by *The New York Times* as one of the Best Illustrated Books of 1970. Among his other books are *The Mystery Beast of Ostergeest, The Orchard Cat, Won't Somebody Play With Me?, The Island of the Skog, The Mystery of the Missing Red Mitten*, and most recently, *Much Bigger Than Martin*. Mr. Kellogg lives in Sandy Hook, Connecticut.